Morning Motivation

With

Matthew Daniels

Volume 1

30 short stories to help motivate and
inspire you.

Introduction

Dear reader, this work which you hold in your hands is a collection of 30 short motivational stories written by myself, Matthew Daniels, with the express intent of inspiring those who read these words. It is my sincere hope and desire that within these pages, you will find everything that you need to pick yourself up from any low state you may be in.

The way in which these stories are constructed are the result of me motivating myself while walking to work each morning. One day, I recorded myself speaking about my motivational thoughts, and I posted the video to social media. The positive response that I received from those closes to me, caused me to continue recording myself and posting it.

Eventually, my talks evolved into the stories you are about to read. It warms my heart to able to share some of my deepest thoughts, insecurities, fears, hopes, dreams, and aspirations with all of you, via my Morning Motivation with Matthew Daniels short stories.

To everyone who may come across these words, may your name live on forever, and may your memory never die. Hotep.

Book One

The Lottery Ticket

Good morning. Good morning. Welcome back to Morning Motivation with Matthew Daniels, and today, I'm gonna tell you guys about, The Lottery Ticket. That's right! The Lottery Ticket. But what is Matthew Daniels talking about? Ummm…

A long, long time ago, somewhere in LaGrange, Tx, there was a young man who had a very bad attitude towards life. This man, who was one of my Ancestors no less, seemed to have no soul at all. He would rob, kill, or steal with no hesitation.

One day, this young man was walking down the street, when he saw a small old lady walking towards the store with a lottery ticket in her hand. Assuming she were headed to go cash in a winning ticket, he rushed over to take it.

"Give me that, old woman." He said, snatching the ticket from her frail hand.

The old woman stood in shock, as the young man began to walk away.

"Young man." She called, still in shock. "Will you really take what is mine, as if it is yours? Will you really do such wickedness?"

"I will, and I have." The young man said, "And if you bother me again, I will do much more wickedness than that."

The old woman gestured her hand as if to submit, and the young man turned to walk away. Then, under her breath she said, "This day, young man, you will learn to do good."

The young man cashed the lottery ticket and walked out of the store. Once outside, he encountered a man who he wanted to beat and rob. The young man raised his hand to strike the man, and when he did, he was instantly back inside of the store, cashing the lottery ticket.

Confused, he took his money and ran out of the store. Seeing the old woman, he ran towards her asking her what she had done. She explained that since he took her lottery ticket, he was cursed to continue going back in time, every time he attempted to do wickedness.

The young man, angered by this, swung to hit the old woman, and instantly, he was back in the store cashing the lottery ticket. The young man tried perhaps a thousand attempts to last longer than that one day without being wicked, and he failed every time.

Finally, fully broken, the young man cashed the lottery ticket, walked out of the store, and gave the money to the old woman. At that moment, the curse was broken, and the young man was no longer wicked.

And so, the Morning Motivation of today is, The Lottery Ticket.

Sometimes, our journey in life has not been problem free. Some of us, most of us, dare I say all of us, have done things, said things, and thought things, that if we're being honest, were not good, right, nor acceptable.

There is no shame in those things which taught us and made us who we are. However, there are some behaviors which we must let die. Do not get caught in a cycle of wickedness. You can break free at any moment. How? By simply doing that which is good.

And remember, you are awesome, you are amazing, you are wonderful, and you are great. And you, are gonna change the world. I just hope I'm still alive to see it, family.

I'm out. Good morning.

Book Two

The Storyteller

Good morning. Good morning. Welcome back to Morning Motivation with Matthew Daniels, and today, I'm gonna tell you guys about, The Storyteller. That's right! The Storyteller. But what is Matthew Daniels talking about? Ummm...

A long, long time ago, there was a man who lived alone at the foot of an active volcano. Nearby to where this man lived, there was a village. Everyone in the village knew about the man who lived alone at the foot of the volcano, but no one knew his name, where he had come from, or how long he had lived at the foot of the volcano.

All they did know about the man was that he told stories. No one even knew why he would do it. And as peculiar as it sounds, the storyteller would only tell stories if he were given a special crystal.

Whenever the people from the village wanted to hear his stories, they would go to a cave nearby, and pluck the crystals from the walls. They never worried about taking too many crystals, because the cave was magic, and later on, more crystals would grow in the walls.

For every crystal they brought to the storyteller, he would tell them one story. The villagers would sit for hours, until everyone heard their own story, and then they would return to their village.

One day, 3 wicked villagers were talking, and one of them said, "I would imagine that the storyteller has countless amounts of magic crystals in his home at the foot of the volcano. And this is probably his secret to long life. We should go and take the storyteller's crystals, and then it will be us who are immortal."

They all agreed, and they went off to rob the storyteller in the dead of night. Breaking into his home, they caught the storyteller reading a book, and they began to beat him.

"Give us the magic crystals." The wicked villagers demanded.

Bloody, and on the ground, the storyteller cried out, "I have no magic crystals. Where are your parents?"

They beat him more, and said, "You have collected the magic crystals for hundreds of years. What have you done with them?"

"The crystals are not magic." The storyteller replied. "Whenever you go back to your village, I go and place the crystals back inside the walls of the cave. The crystals have no value to me. I only like to tell stories and make the people happy."

Suddenly ashamed, the 3 men ran off and told the villagers what they had done. Horrified, they all ran to the volcano and found the storyteller dead. In unison, all of the people cried out, and God Himself decided to hear their cry.

The storyteller, back in his body, sat upright.

"Gather 'round." He said. "I've got yet another story to tell you. And this one is called, The Storyteller."

And so, the Morning Motivation of today is, The Storyteller.

Today family, I just want to thank everyone who gets motivation from my stories. Thank you for reading, thank you for liking, that you for commenting, thank you for following me, thank you for buying my books, and thank you for donating. Thank you for being you and thank you for motivating me.

And remember, you are awesome, you are amazing, you are wonderful, and you are great. And you, are gonna change the world. I just hope I'm still alive to see it, family.

I'm out. Good morning.

Book Three

The Entitled Son

Good morning. Good morning. Welcome back to Morning Motivation with Matthew Daniels, and today, I'm gonna tell you guys about, The Entitled Son. That's right! The Entitled Son. But what is Matthew Daniels talking about? Ummm...

A long, long time ago, in a land which has long since been submerged beneath the sea, a wealthy father was speaking with his entitled son, and he said, "Before you can claim your inheritance, I will give you a simple task to complete. Go out, and build a home with your own two hands, and once you finish, I will give you your inheritance and my blessings to start your own family."

Wanting nothing more than to get his inheritance and become a man, the son agreed to the terms. The sun, however, was lazy, and prideful. He did not want to build a home, and he thought that since his father was wealthy, he was too good to get dirty building a home.

And so, instead of building a home, he went to the woods and found the home of a man who he heard could perform all different feats of magic and sorcery. Finding the magic man sitting in his hut, and wearing a black cloak, he called out.

"Sir. I need your help."

The entitled son then told the magic man what his father had said, and he offered him half of all that he now possessed, if the magic man would use his magic to build him a house.

The magic man warned the entitled son not to use magic in such a situation, but he would not listen. Shrugging his shoulders, the magic man then began to work his craft.

After he finished, he said, "It is done."

The entitled son then went to see his home and was excited when he saw it. That night, a mighty storm came, and heavy rains poured down on the land. After hours of heavy rain, the entitled son realized that his home was beginning to flood. He noticed that the area which usually would hold back the flood waters was stripped bare of its trees to build his home.

Starting to panic, the entitled son, ran back into the woods to find the magic man. He told the man about his new problem and offered him the other half of his possessions if he used his magic to save his home and stop the rains.

Again, the magic man worked his craft. Once finished, he said, "It is done."

The entitled son went back to his home, and when he did, he noticed that the animals, all different kinds, had entered his home, to escape the rains and the floods, and were destroying it.

The entitled son went back to the magic man a third time and begged for his help, but he had already given the magic man all of his possessions, and he had nothing left to pay with.

"I do not know what to do now." The entitled son said.

The magic man replied, "You simply must do the work yourself to remove the animals, like you should have done the work yourself and built the home."

Reluctantly, the entitled son acknowledged that the magic man was correct and decided to go and do the work himself. As he was leaving the hut, the magic man pulled his cloak down off of his head, and the entitled son saw that the magic man had been his wealthy father the whole time.

And so, the Morning Motivation of today is, The Entitled Son.

In life, we may be tempted at times to take shortcuts or cut corners when we are attempting to do a thing. And when we do, we make things worse. Some things can't be rushed, and they can only manifest properly in the fullness of time.

Today family, I want you to give your hopes and dreams the proper amount of attention. Some hands-on attention. Do not leave the execution of your vision to another.

And remember, you are awesome, you are amazing, you are wonderful, and you are great. And you, are gonna change the world. I just hope I'm still alive to see it, family.

I'm out. Good morning.

Book Four

The Darkest Depths of The Mind

Good morning. Good morning. Welcome back to Morning Motivation with Matthew Daniels, and today, I'm gonna tell you guys about, The Darkest Depths of The Mind. That's right! The Darkest Depths of The Mind. But what is Matthew Daniels talking about? Ummm...

A long, long time ago, there was a young girl who had a very foul mouth. Her mother would always encourage her to use good speech and she would often tell her about Curse Demons, in the hopes she would correct how she spoke.

The Curse Demons, the mother told her, were demons whose names included all of the foul things that the daughter would say.

"You are calling to them, my daughter. And they do not like being called. If they decide to come to you, they will bring along with them, all of the curses you are speaking."

The young girl ignored her mother, and her speech did not improve. In fact, it got worse. I should know. This girl was one of my Ancestors, no less.

One day, as the mother had warned, a family of Curse Demons grew tired of listening to the young girl call them, and they came to take up residence in her mind.

"Since this young girl loves our names so much," the head curse demon said, "and she continues to bother us by calling out to us day and night, let us make our names, all that she can think about."

At once, and in unison, the family of curse demons, from the darkest depths of the young girls mind, began to call out their wretched names as loud as they could.

"I hate you!" One screeched.

"You are worthless!" Yelled another.

"No one loves you!" Someone shouted.

"I wish I were dead!"

"You do not deserve to be loved!"

"You look disgusting!"

"You are nothing!"

The young girl, who was sitting inside of her hut when the curse demons began to cry out, dropped down to her knees, and pressed the palms of her hands to her temples.

"I am nothing." The young girl said about herself. "I look disgusting. I do not deserve to be loved. I am worthless. I wish I were dead."

And from that day on, the young girl began to descend into a very dark place. And the older she got, the more she hated herself.

The young girls mother, after watching her daughters torment for years, learned of a magic way in which she could get the curse demons out of her daughter's mind.

"You are awesome," the mother told her daughter. "You are amazing. You are wonderful. And you are great. And you, are gonna change the world."

The mother repeated this phrase, day in and day out, until the Blessed Spirits, who heard the mother calling their names, showed up, entered the darkest depths of the young girl's mind, and kicked out all of the curse demons. And the girl learned once again how to love herself.

And so, the Morning Motivation of today is, The Darkest Depths of The Mind.

Beware family, of what type of energy you invite into your mind. So many of us become consumed with our hate for others, and our obsession descends us into a state of madness in which the thoughts we begin to have about ourselves, no longer sound like they are our own thoughts.

In life, you sometimes have mental battles. And you will undoubtedly lose at times. But continue to fight, continue to push, and continue to press, and do not give in to the negative thoughts in the darkest depths of your mind.

And remember, you are awesome, you are amazing, you are wonderful, and you are great. And you, are gonna change the world. I just hope I'm still alive to see it, family.

I'm out. Good morning.

Book Five

The Mind Reader

Good morning. Good morning. Welcome back to Morning Motivation with Matthew Daniels, and today, I'm gonna tell you guys about, The Mind Reader. That's right! The Mind Reader. But what is Matthew Daniels talking about? Ummm...

A long, long time ago, in a city which sat at the foot of a mighty mountain, 3 midwives were busy at their craft, helping a new mother to give birth.

As they worked, several curious things took place. One curious occurrence was a wolf which began to howl from off in the distance, at the very same time as the child's head crowned and the new mother cried out.

Also, when the child was born, the 3 midwives all claimed to have seen a veil over her face. This veil, along with the howling wolf, was a sign from the gods that the child was special, and she would have a stronger connection to the powers of the spirit world than normal.

"There are many gifts," the midwife said, "so you must wait for hers to manifest on its own. But do not worry, when her gift shows itself, it will be easy to recognize."

When the new mother left with her child, she told her husband all that took place, and the two of them, in complete amazement, wondered what the gift would be.

One day, when the child was 2 years old, the mother was thinking about what type of soup she would cook for dinner, and her daughter said, "Cook the soup with potatoes in it."

The mother's jaw dropped when she realized her daughter had read her mind. She immediately told her husband and the two of them rejoiced.

"A mind reader!" They exclaimed. "Our daughter is a mind reader!"

Several years passed, and the parents tried to help their daughter strengthen and control her gift. They created training exercises and tests, and every day the daughter would work to read minds.

The daughter continued to come up short, and the parents could not figure out why her gift was no longer working, so they pushed her harder, until the daughter refused to even try. The parents, confused, took the girl back to the 3 midwives and explained their problem.

The head midwife said to the girl, "Child. What were you thinking about when you first read your mother's mind? How did you do it?"

"How?" The girl repeated. "Every night my mother does the same thing. She stands and thinks about which soup to make. I did not read her mind. I only read her habits. I am no mind reader."

And so, the Morning Motivation of today is, The Mind Reader.

In life, we all have a gift. Something special about ourselves. But sometimes we get caught up in the cycle of others, where they try to force us to display a gift which is not ours.

If a fish were taught that his purpose was to fly, and live in the trees, he has just been doomed to fail. And if a bird were taught that he should live in the sea, he would utterly fail to achieve this as well.

And so, it is with humans. Some of you were prepared to go left, and others were prepared to go right. Follow your heart and do not be hindered by the misunderstandings of others.

And remember, you are awesome, you are amazing, you are wonderful, and you are great. And you, are gonna change the world. I just hope I'm still alive to see it, family.

I'm out. Good morning.

Book Six

The Master of Fear

Good morning. Good morning. Welcome back to Morning Motivation with Matthew Daniels, and today, I'm gonna tell you guys about, The Master of Fear. That's right! The Master of Fear. But what is Matthew Daniels talking about? Ummm...

A long, long time ago, 3 brothers were talking about how much they disliked their fathers profession of a farmer.

The eldest son said, "I do not want to be a farmer. I want to be a soldier. However, I am afraid that I might fail at being a soldier, so I will become a farmer like our father."

The middle son said, "I do not want to be a farmer. I want to be a blacksmith. However, I am afraid that I might fail at being a blacksmith, so I will become a farmer like our father."

The youngest son said, "I do not want to be a farmer. I want to go to the farthest ends of the earth and see all there is for me to see. And like you, I am afraid that I might fail. However, I will still try."

In time, the eldest and middle son became farmers, and the youngest son packed his bags and headed in the direction of the setting sun.

With every new land he reached, he learned as much as he could about the people there, treated them fairly and righteously, and he would then write down in his books what he learned and how he found the place.

The youngest son, who was one of my very own Ancestors no less, travelled to land after land until he reached a great body of water. Recalling things, he had learned along the way, he built a boat, crossed the waters after several months, and documented his travels.

He met more people in this new land and he continued to follow the setting sun. Many years passed, and the youngest son, through his travels, amassed great wealth, wisdom beyond measure, and hundreds of books documenting his journey.

One year back home, the father, along with the eldest and middle son, was suffering from a drought. The crops had failed for several years, and the family was near death.

As they suffered, the youngest son came approaching from the East. He saved them from certain death and told them about his travels. They were all astonished, even the youngest son, that his journey had brought him back home.

The eldest and middle son said, "Our youngest brother traveled the entire earth. He is indeed a man with no fear.

The youngest son said, "Only a madman has no fear. I merely became the master of my fear."

And so, the Morning Motivation of today is, The Master of Fear.

So many times, in life, we allow fear to hold us back. Instead of following our hearts, we choose instead, to do that which seems safer and more comfortable.

Not knowing, that many times we are being led into our blessings so that we can become a blessing to others. So today family, I want you to cast your fears aside, and do whatever it is that your heart feels compelled to do.

Do it with all of your might. And once you make it to the top of your personal mountain, be sure to return to where you started and show others how you became the master of fear.

And remember, you are awesome, you are amazing, you are wonderful, and you are great. And you, are gonna change the world. I just hope I'm still alive to see it, family.

I'm out. Good morning.

Book Seven

Be Here Now

Good morning. Good morning. Welcome back to Morning Motivation with Matthew Daniels, and today, I'm gonna tell you guys about, Be Here Now. That's right! Be Here Now. But what is Matthew Daniels talking about? Ummm...

A long, long time ago, back when I was a general manager for a worldwide company called McDonald's, I found out through my training about a concept called, Be Here Now.

In essence, what this means, is that you must strive to give your focus to the situation in front of you, regardless if you have other things fighting for your attention or not.

There may be days, and indeed there were for me, when several unfortunate things might happen. For instance, you may be called in to work one morning at 4 am, because your opening manager has called out.

Then, while opening the store yourself, you may notice that the computer is not successfully connecting to the cash registers, and you can not ring up any orders.

On top of that, you soon realize that the oven with which you cook the biscuits, is malfunctioning. So now, you must troubleshoot the oven as well. Also, for some reason, the coffee pot used to brew coffee for the front counter is only brewing half a pot, and you must calibrate the machine.

So, you have been awakened on your off day, at 4 am, to cover the shift at your store. You are only taking cash transactions, you are writing orders down by hand, and with your free moments, you are running back and forth to the office and backroom, trying to get the system to open the store properly.

You also have pulled the side panel off of the oven, while praying you do not need another motherboard, and a simple "turning it off and on" a few times will get the thing heating up to the correct temperature. And you are painfully telling your customers, some of which only came for a biscuit, that you have no products which require a biscuit, but they can substitute for something else.

At the same time, you have pulled out the coffee makers calibration kit, and you are measuring, brewing, and trying desperately to fix that as well. So now, you have multiple pressing issues that all must be addressed. But depending on your approach, you can make matters better or worse.

McDonald's believed that in such a situation, you must, Be Here Now. You must give your attention to the task in front of you. Systematically solving each problem with minimal confusion. For instance, if I am trying to troubleshoot the computer, but my mind is back at home with my wife, I am more likely to make mistakes.

Or, if I'm trying to calibrate the coffee maker, but my mind is on the customer who just yelled at me over a biscuit, the calibration process will take longer. So, focus on the task in front of you.

And so, the Morning Motivation of today is, Be Here Now.

I know that life is not easy. And I know that sometimes you feel like your world is crumbling. Everything that can go wrong, has gone wrong, and your ship may be sinking. So today, family, I want you to focus on the task in front of you, no matter what task you must do next.

Complete one task first and focus your mind on that. Then orderly, and systematically address the other issues.

And remember, you are awesome, you are amazing, you are wonderful, and you are great. And you, are gonna change the world. I just hope I'm still alive to see it, family.

I'm out. Good morning.

Book Eight
Take No Thought

Good morning. Good morning. Welcome back to Morning Motivation with Matthew Daniels, and today, I'm gonna tell you guys about, Take No Thought. That's right! Take No Thought. But what is Matthew Daniels talking about? Ummm...

A long, long time ago, back when men first began to learn the crafts associated with civilization, two men were going about their normal day when one of them said, "I have an idea. I will go out and make the land better by teaching the crafts associated with civilization to the other living creatures."

His friend thought this was a good and noble idea, so he agreed to go with him. The two men first came to the birds.

"Hotep." The men said. Which means 'Divine Peace' in one of the oldest languages of the earth. "We have come to help you. We will teach you agriculture. We will teach you how to sow and how to reap. That way, you will have food."

Then the birds stared at the two men for a moment and said, "We do not need to sow, neither do we need to reap, in order to have food. Look around you. God has given us all that we need. What you describe sounds like extra work. We are content to let God feed us."

"Very well." The men said.

Next, the two men went to the turtles and said, "Hotep. We have come to help you. We will teach you how to build. That way, you can build homes for yourselves as men do."

The turtles stared at them.

"We do not need to build homes for ourselves. Look around you. God has given us our homes on our backs. What you describe sounds like extra work. We are content to let God shelter us."

"Very well." The men said.

Next, the two men went to the lilies of the field and said, "Hotep. We have come to help you. We will teach you how to create cloth, and we will teach you how to spin. That way you can make clothes for yourselves like men do."

The lilies stared at them.

"We do not need to create cloth and spin to make clothes. Look around you. God has arrayed us already with beauty and glory. What you describe sounds like extra work. We are content to let God clothe us."

"Very well." The men said. And they left.

When the men returned to their village, everyone asked them what they had learned from their journey.

The men answered, "What we learned, we will say unto you now. Take no thought for your life, what ye shall eat, or what ye shall drink; nor yet for your body, what ye shall put on. Is not the life more than meat, and the body than raiment?"

Then, after explaining their travels, all understood exactly what the men meant.

And so, the Morning Motivation of today is, Take No Thought.

Today family, I want you to take one deep breath, and mentally collect all of the things you stress and worry about, and then exhaled it out of your mind. Let's start small. I am here to give you one day.

One day of peace which will unfold into more. Today, family, do not stress, simply do that which is good, and let life happen. Trust me. Stress is nothing but extra work.

And remember, you are awesome, you are amazing, you are wonderful, and you are great. And you, are gonna change the world. I just hope I'm still alive to see it, family.

I'm out. Good morning.

Book Nine

The Wise Scribe

Good morning. Good morning. Welcome back to Morning Motivation with Matthew Daniels, and today, I'm gonna tell you guys about, The Wise Scribe. That's right! The Wise Scribe. But what is Matthew Daniels talking about? Ummm…

A long, long time ago, in a strange land beyond the sea, a poor man was sitting down to dinner with his wife and children, when suddenly, he stopped eating and stood up.

"I am tired of living like this." He exclaimed. "Myself, my wife, and my children all deserve better. I will therefore travel to the mysterious land beyond the mountains, and I will ask the wise scribe, and he fell down humbly before him.

"Oh, wise scribe." The poor man began. "Tell me how I can become successful at my craft."

The wise scribe looked up at the poor man, and said, "How bad do you wish to be successful at your craft?"

The man, taking no time at all to respond, said, "I want this more than I want anything else in this world."

The wise scribe softly nodded his head, as he began to write on the scroll.

"So be it." He said.

As he wrote, dark clouds began to roll in, and the ground began to shake. A thick fog descended upon the poor man, and by some supernatural means, he was transported into the very pages of the scroll where he was forced to live out whatever the wise scribe chose to write.

While imprisoned within the scroll, the poor man found himself the slave of a very wicked man. The wicked man, beat him with sticks, fed him the worst kinds of food, abused the poor mans body, and worked him hard from dusk until dawn.

The poor man lived as a slave for several years, until one day he could not take it anymore. In the middle of the night, the poor man cut off his own hand with a sharp stone in order to escape his chains, and he ran off into the woods.

The poor man ran for several days before happening across the wise scribe. When he saw him, the man dropped down to his knees.

"Why have you done this to me?" He asked the scribe. "Why did you send me to this place? It is horrible here."

The wise scribe looked at him and said, "Do you wish to leave this place?"

The poor man answered, "Oh yes, wise scribe. I want nothing more than to leave this place."

The wise scribe said, "So be it. But remember, in order for you to become successful at your craft, you must want to succeed as bad as you now want to be free. You must truly want it above all else."

Then, the man was back at home with his family, his hand was restored, and he had only been away from his family for a few days.

And so, the Morning Motivation of today is, The Wise Scribe.

Often, we have dreams, goals, ambitions, and desires. We have things we wish to accomplish. However, we do not have the internal drive to see it through until the end. We miss our blessings because we do not want it as bad as we think we do.

You have to want it like the poor man wanted freedom, family. You have to be willing to cut off things and people who are holding you back. And you must get up and push every single day. So today family, go out there and conquer.

And remember, you are awesome, you are amazing, you are wonderful, and you are great. And you, are gonna change the world. I just hope I'm still alive to see it, family.

I'm out. Good morning.

Book Ten

Sent To Preserve Life

Good morning. Good morning. Welcome back to Morning Motivation with Matthew Daniels, and today, I'm gonna tell you guys about, Sent To Preserve Life. That's right! Sent To Preserve Life. But what is Matthew Daniels talking about? Ummm...

A long, long time ago, there was a young man named Joseph, who after turning 17 years old, dreamed a series of dreams, in which it was revealed to him that he would be greater than his father, his mother, and all of his eleven older brothers.

His brothers, who already envied their father's love for Joseph, hated him even more, now that he was dreaming dreams.

These eleven brothers hated Joseph so much, that they conspired to sell him into slavery. And to cover their wickedness, they dipped his coat of many colors in animals blood, and lied to their father, about what happened.

The young man was in turn sold again to an Egyptian who worked in Pharoah's guard. From there, the young man, even though he was wronged, continued to be righteous, and the favor of God stayed on his life.

One day, he was lied on by the wife of his master, because he rejected her wicked advances. For this, he was thrown into Pharoah's prison.

While in prison, the young man, interpreted the dreams of several prisoners, and he eventually interpreted a dream for Pharoah himself. A dream, that God had used, to raise the young man from his position in life as a slave and captive.

With wisdom from God, the young man saved the land of Egypt from seven years of famine, enriched Pharoah even more than he already was, and became the second most powerful man in the whole land of Egypt.

Ironically, this same famine crippled his family back home, and they were forced to travel to Egypt to find food.

Once in Egypt, the eleven brothers were forced to stand before their brother they had sold off into slavery so many years ago. The young man, Joseph, recognized his brothers, but they did not recognize him.

Using this to his advantage, Joseph played several tricks on them, and had them go home, and then return back to Egypt again.

Soon, Joseph could stand it no longer and he burst out in tears.

"I am Joseph; doth my father yet live?" He cried out.

His brothers, suddenly afraid of his power and their past wickedness, could not answer him.

And Joseph said, "Come near to me, I pray you. I am Joseph your brother, whom ye sold into Egypt. Now therefore be not grieved, nor angry with yourselves, that ye sold me hither; for God did send me before you to preserve life."

And in that moment, Joseph's dreams were his reality.

And so, the Morning Motivation today is, Sent To Preserve Life.

We all want a mission in life. A purpose, a goal, a journey to take. And most of us, genuinely want to succeed, so that we can help those around us. Indeed, it is a noble cause being sent to preserve life.

But there are no guarantees where you might get sent. It may be hard, it may be long, it may be steep, it may be wide. It may break you down or build you up. Leave you for dead or forge you into steel.

Sometimes family, you must be prepared to dig deep, and walk through the valley of the shadow of death. If there's a chance that when it's all over, you were being Sent To Preserve Life.

And remember, you are awesome, you are amazing, you are wonderful, and you are great. And you, are gonna change the world. I just hope I'm still alive to see it, family.

I'm out. Good morning.

Book Eleven

The 5 Why's

Good morning. Good morning. Welcome back to Morning Motivation with Matthew Daniels, and today, I'm gonna tell you guys about, The 5 Why's. That's right! The 5 Why's. But what is Matthew Daniels talking about? Ummm...

A long, long time ago, I was a General Manager for a worldwide company called McDonald's. McDonald's rarely hired in managers off the street. It was a practice of theirs, instead, to promote from within.

So, I began my journey as a grill cook. And within four short years, I was running my own store. During my training, to become a general manager, I came across something that was called in the curriculum, The 5 Why's.

Someone, somewhere, at some point in time, had determined that in order to get to the root cause of a problem, a manager must ask the question "why", at least 5 times. For example: You notice on your shift that a customer's burger was not cooked thoroughly, and it was served raw.

Ok. Why?

Perhaps the grill did not cook the patty properly.

Ok. Why?

Perhaps the temperature is correct, but the timer is off.

Ok. Why?

Perhaps someone changed the timer and changed the cook temperature in order to make patties faster. Then, they changed the cooking temperature back but forgot to change the cooking timer back.

Ok. Why?

Perhaps the grill cook was behind and needed to cut corners in order to get caught up.

Ok. But, why?

Perhaps for the past few days the manager on duty was sending people on break right before the rush.

Now, after the fifth why, you see that the root cause is the manager from another shift. They need to be coached. However, had you not investigated, perhaps you would have immediately yelled at the current grill cook, and they would have done nothing wrong.

And so, the Morning Motivation of today is, The 5 Why's.

Beware of jumping to conclusions family, and steer clear of rushing to judgement. More often then not, in order to properly assess a situation, you must take time to think your way through the nuances.

Quite often, things are not what they might first appear to be. As you go on this journey called life today, and something inconvenient or unexpected comes up, remember this story, and remember The Five Why's.

Then, use your intelligence to navigate you to a successful end.

And remember, you are awesome, you are amazing, you are wonderful, and you are great. And you, are gonna change the world. I just hope I'm still alive to see it, family.

I'm out. Good morning.

Book Twelve

You Reap What You Sow

Good morning. Good morning. Welcome back to Morning Motivation with Matthew Daniels, and today, I'm gonna tell you guys about, You Reap What You Sow. That's right! You Reap What You Sow. But what is Matthew Daniels talking about? Ummm...

A long, long time ago, in the area we know of as Spain today, a mother and daughter were working to collect the harvest, when the daughter asked her mother why did the harvest come at the same time each year. The mother smiled and said, "A long, long time ago, when the earth was first formed, there was no green thing upon the land. All was desolate, dirt, dust, sand, and rock."

The mother then went on to explain how God created a being named Annunan to seed the earth with all forms of vegetation life. Knowing his mission, once created, Annunan flew down to earth to complete his task.

As soon as he came close to the ground; trees, plants flowers, and grain, and all sorts of plant life sprang forth from it. Annunan then proceeded to fly around the earth and seed it with life. He did not realize it, but the further he went away from any spot on the ground, the less effect his powers seemed to have.

Annunan soon circled the entire earth, and when he returned to the spot where he had begun, he saw that the earth was cold and dying. So, he revived the earth, and began the same journey again, following his path, to save the dying earth.

And again, when he reached the starting point, earth was cold and dying. So, determined to complete his mission and seed the entire earth, Annunan began his journey yet again.

"And he has done this." The mother said. "Until this very day."

Amazed, the daughter asked her mother why did Annunan not just give up and stop circling the earth. The mother said it was because Annunan was created to seed the earth. If he ever stopped seeding the earth, and the earth died, then Annunan would die too. So, Annunan needs to seed the earth, just as bad as the earth needs Annunan to seed it. Annunan sows life, and so Annunan reaps life.

And so, the Morning Motivation of today is, You Reap What You Sow.

In life family, we all have a purpose. And that purpose is sometimes intertwined with others. There are things which we may need on earth, things we can not acquire alone. And it is only when we work in tandem with others, that all of us succeed.

It is my unending hope that these stories of mine which you have now found, are sowing into you all of the things you need to be the best you. I sow into you positivity, strength, courage, hope, patience, wisdom, and an unbreakable will. I sow these things into you all, much like Annunan sows into the earth, for without you, there is no me.

And remember, you are awesome, you are amazing, you are wonderful, and you are great. And you, are gonna change the world. I just hope I'm still alive to see it, family.

I'm out. Good morning.

Book Thirteen

The Christmas List

Good morning. Good morning. Welcome back to Morning Motivation with Matthew Daniels, and today, I'm gonna tell you guys about, The Christmas List. That's right! The Christmas List. But what is Matthew Daniels talking about? Ummm...

A long, long time ago, a sad mother was sitting alone inside of her home, and the idea entered into her mind to bake a cake for her two daughters. Now both of this sad mother's daughters were grown, and they were living in their own homes, going about life as they saw fit.

"Yes." The sad mother said. "I will bake my daughters a cake. Once they taste my delicious cake, they will forgive me for our most recent disagreement."

Smiling, the mother began to bake, and she put her heart and soul into the cake, along with all of the other ingredients. Such as eggs, milk, flour, etc...

Once the cake was finished the sad mother clapped her hands with glee. She then ran over to the phone and called her eldest daughter. Lovingly, she invited her daughter to come and taste her cake.

The daughter, still mad over their most recent disagreement said, "Whenever I need you, you are never there. Since you could not give me what I asked for, I do not want to taste your cake."

Then the daughter hung up the phone.

Sad, hurt, and holding back tears, the mother called her second daughter. Lovingly, she invited her daughter to come and taste her cake. The second daughter responded much like the first, and then hung up the phone.

The mother placed the cake on a tabletop in her home and laid down to go to sleep. That night, death came for the mother, and death carried her swiftly in her sleep to the land of the ancestors.

The next day, when the daughter's heard about what happened, they broke out in tears, and rushed to their mother's house. Bursting through the front, the first thing they saw was the cake their mother had made them. The sight was too much to bear and both daughters cried for hours.

Once they were all cried out, the two daughters began to sort through their mother's things. As they did, they came across a folded-up piece of paper in her purse. Pulling it out slowly to examine it, the two daughters realized that it was a Christmas list their mother had made.

After reading it, both daughters said, "Our mother did not give us what we asked for, and this led to our disagreement, but our mother only refused so that she could get us all special Christmas gifts. We have wasted our final moments with our mother for nothing."

And both daughters were sad.

And so, the Morning Motivation of today is, The Christmas List.

No one knows how much time we have with our loved ones. Death, for whatever reason comes for us all. And all too often, we miss out on moments on earth over small, trivial, and insignificant things. Today family, I want you to cherish every moment, every breath, every smile, and every interaction. And make sure that the people you love, know that you love them.

And remember, you are awesome, you are amazing, you are wonderful, and you are great. And you, are gonna change the world. I just hope I'm still alive to see it, family.

I'm out. Good morning.

Book Fourteen

The Mission From God

Good morning. Good morning. Welcome back to Morning Motivation with Matthew Daniels, and today, I'm gonna tell you guys about, The Mission From God. That's right! The Mission From God. But what is Matthew Daniels talking about? Ummm...

A long, long time ago, somewhere near the area now know as the Congo, a young man was walking through the rainforest alone, when off in the distance, he could see the figure of a man who seemed to stand 10 ft tall.

Being more intrigued than afraid, the young man headed over for a closer look. The 10 ft tall figure, slowly turned around as the young man approached. Shocked, the young man could see that the figure was closer to 15 ft tall, and his face shined like the sun.

The figure called out to my ancestor by name, and his voice came forth like a thunder. The young man fell down to the ground in awe.

"Oh, Great Mysterious One." He prayed, realizing this figure was there on behalf of God. "Aluk Aluka."

Which is to say, "My hands are yours."

The Messenger from God instructed the young man in all that he must do. And he showed him bits and pieces of future events, but he did not tell the young man, 'how', he was supposed to accomplish his task. And when he tried to ask, the Messenger was gone, and he was again alone in the rainforest.

The young man ran home and told his family and friends of his assignment, but they all mocked him.

"Why would God choose you?" They scoffed.

The man ignored them all and began to attempt his mission. Day after day, and year after year, he continued to fail. It got so bad, family, the young man began to doubt his encounter with the Messenger himself.

"Was I really chosen?" He wondered.

The young man became an old man. An old man with a wife and 3 children. All of which watched this man try and fail but never give up. One day, the young man turned old man died. He died without ever accomplishing his task.

When he reached the other side of life, he saw the 15 ft Messenger with the shining face.

"Oh, Great Mysterious One." He prayed. "I am sorry. I failed you. I humbly accept my fate."

"Do not be sorry." The Messenger said. "You did not fail. You did amazing."

Then, the Messenger waved his hands, and showed the man events upon the earth. The man saw that his children had taken up his cause and completed the mission for him.

"Your true mission." The Messenger revealed. "Was to inspire them."

And so, the Morning Motivation of today is, The Mission From God.

Sometimes we can not see all of the details to the big picture in life. And sometimes, we remain inactive because of this. Do not make that mistake today, family. Today, you must seize the moment, and try to do that which you are on earth to do. If you fail, try again. If you fail again, you should try again.

Because who knows, maybe the mission from God is to pave the way for someone else.

And remember, you are awesome, you are amazing, you are wonderful, and you are great. And you, are gonna change the world. I just hope I'm still alive to see it, family.

I'm out. Good morning.

Book Fifteen

The Man Who Questioned the Phoenix

Good morning. Good morning. Welcome back to Morning Motivation with Matthew Daniels, and today, I'm gonna tell you guys about, The Man Who Questioned the Phoenix. That's right! The Man Who Questioned the Phoenix. But what is Matthew Daniels talking about? Ummm...

A long, long time ago, in the lands that we call Arabia today, a man was out hunting, trying to capture some game to feed his family. This man was one of my ancestors no less, and this is how I know what took place.

While hunting, the man came upon a gazelle grazing, and he positioned himself with his bow and arrow. Just when he was about to shoot, a large snake, who was hiding nearby, bit the man on the leg.

"Ahhh!" The man cried out, recklessly releasing his arrow, and missing his prey.

Looking down to see what bit him, he saw the snake. Afraid, the man ran off as fast as he could, trying to escape.

As the man ran, he saw a huge bird off in the distance, and the bird seemed to be on fire. Forgetting about the snake, the man ran over to the bird.

"Sir." The man said. "What kind of bird are you, that you are on fire, but do not burn."

The Phoenix looked down at the man and said, "I am the Phoenix, and I am the only one of my kind. And I am not on fire, this is simply how I look."

Amazed, the man asked, "Where did you come from, Phoenix?"

"I have just emerged from the corpse of my predecessor. But in fact, I am my predecessor, and I am also my predecessor's predecessor. There is only one Phoenix, who is reborn every 1,500 years."

The man looked around and saw the corpse of the predecessor, mixed with frankincense and myrrh, as if it were being shaped into something.

"What are you doing with the corpse?" He asked.

"I am preparing it for the trip. Once it is ready, I will carry it down to Egypt, where we were first born on earth, I will place him on the altar in the Temple of Amen-Ra, and I will go off to live my 1,500 years."

Intrigued, the man asked, "Can I travel with you?"

"If you wish." The Phoenix replied.

Once in Egypt, and after the Phoenix had offered the corpse on the altar, the man looked down at his leg and he wondered what happened to his snakebite.

"Hmmm. What happened to my snakebite?" He asked.

"Finally." The Phoenix replied. "You have asked a good question. The snakebite is still on your body. And your body is still in Arabia, lying under a tree. The snake that bit you was poisonous. You died while running away.

The man began to panic. "If I am dead, why am I here, and not in the land of ghosts?"

"Because you are lucky." The Phoenix said. "I have within me the power of resurrection, but you must ask for it on your own."

"Resurrect me." The man cried. "Give me another chance to be with my family."

"So be it." The Phoenix said. "Since you asked."

Instantly, the man was back in his body, and he was healed. He jumped up and ran home as fast as he could.

And so, the Morning Motivation of today is, The Man Who Questioned the Phoenix.

Remember to be aware of your surroundings family, and contemplate how you ended up in any situation you are in. When in need of a solution, you must know the right questions to ask. At times, we concern ourselves with things that will not help us reach the next level. So today, I want you to analyze everything about your current situation, and then utilize the resources at your disposal, to become the best you.

And remember, you are awesome, you are amazing, you are wonderful, and you are great. And you, are gonna change the world. I just hope I'm still alive to see it, family.

I'm out. Good morning.

Book Sixteen

The Brothers Who Debated the Meaning of Life

Good morning. Good morning. Welcome back to Morning Motivation with Matthew Daniels, and today, I'm gonna tell you guys about, The Brothers Who Debated the Meaning of Life. That's right! The Brothers Who Debated the Meaning of Life. But what is Matthew Daniels talking about? Ummm...

A long, long time ago, in a land where the sun never sets, 3 brothers were in a heated debate about the meaning of life.

The eldest brother said, "The meaning of life is simple. We are here to acquire wealth, and possessions, and live the best we can while we are here. And you two fools are wrong."

The middle brother said, "The meaning of life is simple. We are here to produce children. As many as we can and populate the earth while we are here. And you two fools are wrong."

The youngest brother said, "The meaning of life is simple. We are here to prepare ourselves for the life after death, and spend day and night in communion with God, and isolate ourselves from others, while we are here. And you two fools are wrong."

The 3 brothers then argued about whose answer was correct. They argued so ferociously, that out of nowhere, all 3 brothers charged at each other. Just when they were about to collide, all 3 brothers went unconscious, and blacked out.

When they awoke, they were inside of a cave with a massive fire burning in the center, and a giant was seated in front of the exit. Instantly, the 3 brothers, who were my very own ancestors no less, began to debate and argue about how they ended up in that place.

Just then, a voice bellowed from the walls of the cave as if the cave itself were speaking, and said, "How did you get here?"

Afraid, the eldest brother called. "We do not know how we got here."

"Why did you come?" The voice questioned.

"We do not know!" The middle brother called back.

"If you do not know 'how' you got here." The voice bellowed. "And you do not know 'why' you came. How then do you debate it?"

"I suppose we cannot." The youngest brother called back.

"Likewise," the voice bellowed. "You do not know 'how' you were given life. And you do not know 'why'. So how then do you brothers debate the meaning of life? Perhaps all 3 of you are correct for yourselves. Perhaps meaning is to be found in the 'how' and the 'why'."

Again the 3 brothers blacked out, and when they awoke, they were at home in the land where the sun never sets, and they never debated the meaning of life again.

And so, the Morning Motivation of today is, The Brothers Who Debated the Meaning of Life.

Who cares, family, if anyone at all agrees with you about the meaning of your life? We all came to this earth confused. And we have relied on others, and that voice inside of ourselves, which sounds like us, but does not appear to be us, to guide us along life's journey.

Indeed, we were not all created to be clones of each other. All walking, talking, and thinking the same. Some build, some teach, some defend, and some research. And it is amazing to me, how much seemingly different purposes in the micro-version of things, can all fall in sync together, when we look at the big picture.

We are headed to the same end family; we're just traveling different roads. Be you on your journey. The authentic you.

And remember, you are awesome, you are amazing, you are wonderful, and you are great. And you, are gonna change the world. I just hope I'm still alive to see it, family.

I'm out. Good morning.

Book Seventeen

The Man Who Lived Many Lives

Good morning. Good morning. Welcome back to Morning Motivation with Matthew Daniels, and today, I'm gonna tell you guys about, The Man Who Lived Many Lives. That's right! The Man Who Lived Many Lives. But what is Matthew Daniels talking about? Ummm…

There once was a man, a long, long time ago, who lived 1,000 different lives. I should know, this man was one of my very own ancestors. When he was young, he would complain about everything. He did not like his family, he did not like how he looked, he did not like his siblings, and he did not even like to eat food. The only thing, I am told this man liked, was the ability to 'not' like a thing.

One day, when he was 10 years old, an evil spirit was passing through the village, and it overheard the child complaining about his life. And so, being a crafty evil spirit, he went in to speak with him.

"Child." The evil spirit said. "I heard you speaking, and it seems as if you do not like your life. Well, if that is the case, I can give you a different life. And all I want in return is your youth."

The child thought about it, and said that he indeed wanted a new life, and he didn't mind the evil spirit taking his youth, because he did not like his youth anyway.

"Very well." The evil spirit said. "Whatever you don't like about your life will change." And then the evil spirit left.

The child looked around, and nothing happened.

"Well." He said. "I don't like that evil spirit."

As soon as he had finished his sentence, everything around him went black, and in an instance, when he could see again, he was in a strange land which he had never seen before. And he noticed his body had aged one year.

Suddenly afraid, the child said, "I do not like this strange place."

Again, all went dark, and in an instant, he was in yet another strange land, and there were lions resting nearby. His body had again aged one year. The child cried out, and excited the lions, who charged directly at him. The child thought how much he disliked being eaten alive, and he was taken instantly to a far away land of ice and death.

The child changed lives like this until he was 100 years old. As he took his last breath, he thought, I do not like death. And he instantly went to another life, to take his last breath.

And it was in this state, that my ancestor lived his many lives. Each life on the brink of death. Dying each day but being born to die again tomorrow. He lived like that until God himself came and saved him from his curse of death.

And so, the Morning Motivation of today is, The Man Who Lived Many Lives.

In life, we sometimes can get lost in a cycle of trying to reinvent ourselves to find the best version of us that the world will accept. And while doing this, trying to please others, we lose ourselves in the process. We become characters and avatars, walking through life in a costume with a mask on. The real us dying a young death and the manufactured us dying a perpetual death with each new upgrade.

But luckily for you, you have found my books. And since I know how my ancestor was saved, I know that you will be saved too.

And remember, you are awesome, you are amazing, you are wonderful, and you are great. And you, are gonna change the world. I just hope I'm still alive to see it, family.

I'm out. Good morning.

Book Eighteen

It's Always Been You

Good morning. Good morning. Welcome back to Morning Motivation with Matthew Daniels, and today, I'm gonna tell you guys about, It's Always Been You. That's right! It's Always Been You. But what is Matthew Daniels talking about? Ummm...

A long, long time ago, in a land whose name I can not properly pronounce, there lived a man and woman who were madly in love. So much so in fact, that everyone said a love like there's was impossible for anyone else to experience.

The man did any and everything for the woman. And likewise, the woman did all for the man. These two enjoyed a marriage of pure bliss for 65 years, and then, the man, doing what all men must eventually do, passed on to the realm of the ancestors.

In the afterlife, the man stood before God to be judged. His thoughts, actions, and deeds were considered, and the man was deemed righteous, and worthy of an afterlife in paradise.

"My Lord and my God." The man called out, before entering into paradise. "I love my beautiful and loving wife more than any husband has ever loved his wife. Please, I pray you, send me back to earth. I will gladly forego paradise for her."

"So be it." God said.

And with that, the man was sent back to earth as a newborn child. And before he was old enough to find his wife, she too had passed on, and he realized his grievous mistake.

The man then began to search for his wife, hoping that she would choose to come back to him as well. The man searched and searched until he again passed away.

Once again standing before God, the man asked if God had seen his wife.

"Yes." God said. "And like you, she went back to earth to find you."

Missing his beautiful and loving wife even more, he asked God to send him back to earth, and God agreed.

This man and this woman, searched for each other through countless lifetimes and over the course of countless years, and their love for one another never wavered nor faltered.

With every new life that they lived, their hearts and their souls, drew them ever closer, like a powerful magnet.

Until one day, the man entered a city, the name of which I can't properly pronounce, and he was going about searching for his wife. As he searched, a woman slowly walked up behind him.

"What are you searching for so diligently, sir?" She asked, in a voice familiar to the man.

Quickly turning around, the mans heart leapt from his chest.

"You!" He cried. "I am searching for you! It's always been you!"

And so, the Morning Motivation of today is, It's Always Been You.

You, family, are someone's special person. Someone, somewhere, has been searching for you. And that person wants to love you for you and complete you. And you, family, have been searching for them.

Once you find one another again, be sure to love as hard as you can. Who knows when you'll get a second chance? And as odd as it sounds, I too, have been looking for you for a thousand years. I wanted to remind you that there is only one you.

And remember, you are awesome, you are amazing, you are wonderful, and you are great. And you, are gonna change the world. I just hope I'm still alive to see it, family.

I'm out. Good morning.

Book Nineteen

The Owl and The Hourglass

Good morning. Good morning. Welcome back to Morning Motivation with Matthew Daniels, and today, I'm gonna tell you guys about, The Owl and The Hourglass. That's right! The Owl and The Hourglass. But what is Matthew Daniels talking about? Ummm...

A long, long time ago, somewhere deep in the outback's of what we now call Australia, back when that region was teeming with life, there were rivers, lakes, woods, and wildlife. Also, there lived there a young woman, who was as self-conscious as a person could be. She did not think anything at all about herself was unique, intriguing, inspiring, or special. In fact, most days, she wished that she had never been born.

One day, feeling down as she often did, the young woman ran off into the woods, trying to put as much distance between herself and her torturous thoughts, as possible. She ran and ran, until the sound of self-loathing faded away, and transformed into the sounds of the night.

The young woman stopped to rest beneath a tree, and there she sat, with her knees pulled up to her chest, balling her eyes out. As was her habit, the self-conscious young woman began to lament her lot in life and wished yet again that she had never been born.

Sitting in the tree, just above her head was a large grey owl, with 2 large black eyes.

"Be careful what you wish for child." The Owl said. "Your words have power."

"I do not care, Owl." She responded. "I do indeed wish that I had never been born."

The owl looked directly at her and then transformed into a frightening witch.

"Well then, child." The witch said. "You shall have your wish."

The witch then made a large hourglass appear. She told the young woman that when the hourglass ran out of sand, she would die a horrible and painful death.

Horrified, the young woman screeched. "I didn't ask you to kill me!"

"Yet," the witch said. "You will soon be dead."

The witch then turned back into an owl and flew away. The young woman turned and ran home as fast as she could, thinking of ways to save herself. Reaching her family, she told them her fate, and they all embraced her and burst into tears. They all prayed and begged, but the hourglass would not stop.

When the last grain of sand fell, the young woman cried out, and her soul rose from her flesh. Time seemed to stop moving, and the young woman could see the owl.

"Why do you cry out, child?" The owl asked.

"Because I want to live." The young woman yelled.

"So be it." The Owl said. "You shall live."

From that day forward, the young woman learned to find the joy in the life, and she healed her mind and spirit, and she never forgot about the owl and the hourglass.

And so, the Morning Motivation of today is, The Owl and The Hourglass.

Today family, is precious. This day, this second, this very moment in time, you exist with endless possibilities to go out and seek happiness and joy. Yes, problems may arise, but why does a problem deserve more energy than peace? Can't one simply solve the problem while at peace? Must we solve the problem while being tossed to and fro?

Life will never be easy, this seems true. However, we can find that thing which we are on earth to do, and we can spend every single moment, like this moment right here, doing that very thing. Because you never know when you will be visited by The Owl and The Hourglass.

And remember, you are awesome, you are amazing, you are wonderful, and you are great. And you, are gonna change the world. I just hope I'm still alive to see it, family.

I'm out. Good morning.

Book Twenty

The Planet is Big and Life is Short

Good morning. Good morning. Welcome back to Morning Motivation with Matthew Daniels, and today, I'm gonna tell you guys about, The Planet is Big and Life is Short. That's right! The Planet is Big and Life is Short. But what is Matthew Daniels talking about? Ummm...

A long, long time ago, in a land which has long since been submerged under the sea, there lived a boy who had become a man. Now this man, as a boy, always told himself that one day he would marry a local girl in his town, who was the same age as him.

Once he had become a man, and completed all of the necessary rites of passage, he began to work at acquiring the dowry for his wife, which was 75 cows and 25 buckets of grain.

Wanting nothing more in this world than to marry this woman, the man took no time at all acquiring the dowry.

He then said, "I have the dowry, yes. But I do not have a home. I will now get a home, and then get my wife."

The man then spent his savings on a nice home, he furnished it well, then he tried again to earn the dowry. Again, he quickly saved the dowry.

He then said, "I have the dowry and the home yes, But I have no land on which to raise our children and earn my living. I will now get land, and then I will get my wife."

The man, determined to have his wife, bought his land, and tried yet again to save the dowry.

Again, he saved it, and again he said, "I have the dowry, the home, and the land, yes, but I do not know how to defend it. I will first go and train with the warriors. Once I can defend my wife, my children, my home, and my land, then I will get my wife."

The man then went to the train with the warriors. As he trained, a war broke out. He was forced to go and defend his people. He fought valiantly, and he was killed. The woman who was to be his wife, cried out in agony at her loss.

The man, still determined to have his wife, stood before God Himself, and he explained to God how much he loved the woman, and he begged God to give him another chance to have her.

God then looked down at the man and said, "I gave you time with her as a child, and I gave you time with her as a man. It was you who chose to wait to enjoy your time with her. Death, my child, is one thing which can not be undone. You should have loved her while you were alive."

And so, the Morning Motivation of today is, The Planet is Big and Life is Short.

That which you wish to do, you should get about doing it. Today, family, do not make the mistake of thinking you will be here tomorrow.

Death will one day come for us all, so while you are alive, make sure that you live. Love those which you love, go where you wish to go, do that which you wish to do, and never mistake procrastination for proper planning.

God has given you something to love while you are here. Find it, love it, and never let it go. And after we die, I will see you on the other side.

And remember, you are awesome, you are amazing, you are wonderful, and you are great. And you, are gonna change the world. I just hope I'm still alive to see it, family.

I'm out. Good morning.

Book Twenty-One

Where Do Butterflies Come From

Good morning. Good morning. Welcome back to Morning Motivation with Matthew Daniels, and today, I'm gonna tell you guys about, Where Do Butterflies Come From. That's right! Where Do Butterflies Come From. But what is Matthew Daniels talking about? Ummm…

A long, long time ago, somewhere in West Africa, one of my ancestors asked his father, "Father, where do butterflies come from?"

The father, looked down at his son and replied, "Where do butterflies come from? Well, a long, long time ago, somewhere in the east, when God had finished his creation, the caterpillar had begun to be displeased with his lot in life.

Indeed, as he crawled around on his belly, he was easy prey for any predator who enjoyed how he tasted. He would often wish that he could fly away from all of his enemies on the ground, but unfortunately, that was not his fate.

He had begun life as a caterpillar, and he would remain one until he died, probably in the belly of a predator.

The caterpillar, lived with his fate, until one day, he heard of a man which had come nearby. And this man, it was said, had the power to give sight to the blind, raise the dead, cause the lame to walk, and the mute to speak.

"Surely." The caterpillar said. "If this man can do all of that, he can easily cause me to fly."

The caterpillar went to a mound, on which the man was speaking, and he poured out his heart to the man, and he presented his case. He told him how he had been treated, and how he was nothing but food for his enemies.

His mother, father, sister, and brother, all gone too soon.

"Please, sir." The caterpillar begged. "Save me from my plight."

The man listened to the caterpillar's story intently.

And then he said, "You have traveled here to tell me all of this. You must really believe that I can help you."

"I do believe." The caterpillar said. "If you can make the lame to walk, you can make me to fly."

As soon as the caterpillar ended his sentence, a strange substance began to encase his entire body. At peace, and not afraid, the caterpillar allowed himself to be wrapped inside of the cocoon.

In the proper process of time, the caterpillar emerged from his cocoon as a beautiful butterfly, and he flapped his wings in shock. And from that day forth, all caterpillars, in the proper process of time, would transform into a butterfly.

"And so," the father said to his son. "That is where butterflies come from."

And so, the Morning Motivation of today is, Where Do Butterflies Come From.

Today family, remember that we all have an origin story, a series of events that brought us to where we are in life. And often, our journey has sometimes knocked us down, and made us prey for our enemies. You may be trying to become the best version of yourself, and soar high as an eagle or a hawk, but you may not know how.

You have to see yourself as a butterfly, family, and do the work to achieve it. And also, you must believe, family. You must believe that you will one day fly.

And remember, you are awesome, you are amazing, you are wonderful, and you are great. And you, are gonna change the world. I just hope I'm still alive to see it, family.

I'm out. Good morning.

Book Twenty-Two
Thou Art The Man

Good morning. Good morning. Welcome back to Morning Motivation with Matthew Daniels, and today, I'm gonna tell you guys about, Thou Art The Man. That's right. Thou Art The Man. But what is Matthew Daniels talking about? Ummm…

A long, long time ago, in a nation along the Mediterranean Sea, a king named David had arisen from his bed and walked out upon the roof of his house. From there, he could see a very beautiful woman.

"Who is that woman?" The King inquired of the people around him.

"Is that not Bathsheba?" One said. "The daughter of Eliam, and the wife of Uriah the Hittite?"

Indeed, it was, but the King did not care. He ordered his men to get her for him, and the King took her to his bed chambers. And then, after his wicked act, the King sent the woman home. Because she was forced to do this, the woman was purified from uncleanliness, but King David had sinned greatly.

In time, the woman revealed that she was pregnant, and the child was the King's child, because her husband, Uriah, was off at war fighting in the name of King David and the Nation of Israel.

To hide his wickedness, the King tried to convince Uriah to lie with his wife, so that Uriah would think the child was his, but Uriah wanted to go back to war and defend his people.

The King, sinking further into his wickedness, sent Uriah to the front lines of the war, and gave his generals letters, commanding them to let Uriah be killed.

After this, God sent a prophet to the King.

"There were 2 men in one city." The prophet said. "One rich and one poor. The rich man had many flocks and herds, but the poor man had nothing, save one little ewe lamb. This lamb grew up with the man, and with his children. The lamb ate what the poor man ate and drank what he and his children drank. The lamb would lay on the mans chest, and indeed, it was like a daughter unto him."

"And one day a traveler came to the rich man, and instead of taking from his own flocks to dress for the traveler, he took the poor man's lamb, killed it, and dressed it for his traveler."

The King became angered.

"As the Lord liveth. Whoever has done such evil in this land, that man will surely die. And that man shall restore the lamb fourfold because that man did this thing and had no pity."

The prophet pointed at the King and said, "Thou art the man! Thus, saith the Lord…"

The prophet then told the King what would befall his kingdom. He was told that the child of Bathsheba would die, and he would have to fight wars all of his days and have no peace.

Also, his kingdom, would be torn in two. The King begged God to reconsider, but it was too late. All that the prophet said would happen, did happen.

And so, the Morning Motivation of today is, Thou Art The Man.

Today family, remember that your actions have consequences. There are times when an action may be wrong, but we still do it because we think we can hide our wickedness. Then, to keep our indiscretions secret, we do and say more wickedness to cover our tracks.

This behavior can lead you to the point of no return, and the reality is, you can lose all that you have built. So, it is better, I would assume, to not do wickedness in the first place, as opposed to hiding and covering it up. Accountability is real, and your wrongs can't always be made right. Beware of what you say and do. Your today will create your tomorrow.

And remember, you are awesome, you are amazing, you are wonderful, and you are great. And you, are gonna change the world. I just hope I'm still alive to see it, family.

I'm out. Good morning.

Book Twenty-Three

Mom's Pajamas

Good morning. Good morning. Welcome back to Morning Motivation with Matthew Daniels, and today, I'm gonna tell you guys about, Mom's Pajamas. That's right! Mom's Pajamas. But what is Matthew Daniels talking about? Ummm...

A long, long time ago, in the area we now call Czechoslovakia today, a rich woman was reading in her personal garden, when a messenger approached her running full speed.

"My... apologizes... ma'am." The messenger said, out of breath. "I bring word from your family in the south. "Your sister, ma'am. She is sick. Your family asks that you come at once."

The rich woman wasted no time at all. She leaped from her seat in the garden and sprang into action. With the help of her family, she loaded up her pack animals and wagons with enough provisions, so that she may live with her family in the south for several years if she wished.

While on the road, the rich woman and her group were traveling through dangerous territory cautiously, when out of the shadows one night, they were attacked by a band of murderers and thieves. An arrow from the trees began the attack. Blood being spilled before any words or warnings.

The family of the rich woman fought with courage and honor, but the bandits were a bloodthirsty bunch who could only survive through plunder.

From inside of a covered wagon, the rich woman knew that she was running out of time.

"These bandits will not stop me from reaching my sister." She declared.

Looking down at the red and white striped pajamas she was wearing, she hugged herself tight, and transferred all of her love, support, comfort, and positive energy into the pajamas. She then changed clothes and placed the pajamas inside of a sack tied to a horse.

"May God guide you to my sister."

The rich woman slapped the horse, and off it went.

As the horse traveled, it lost its way, and turned around. And when it did, the sister of the rich woman passed away, and she moved on to the land of the ancestors.

But as she rose up into heaven, she looked down and saw the horse. And she also saw her daughter, who was grieving hard the loss of her mother.

The sister then went down and led the horse to her daughter.

"You now need this more than me." She said.

The daughter, seeing the horse one day, but not knowing from whence it had come, she walked over to it and looked inside of the sack.

"Hmmm." She said, seeing the pajamas. "Those look nice."

Reaching down, she grabbed them. And when she did, all of the rich woman's love, support, comfort, and positive energy entered her body, and for a moment, she was able to speak with her mother.

She told her to be strong, and that she was ok, and that she loved her forever.

The daughter thought about how the gift meant for her mother had provided exactly what she needed, exactly 'when' she needed it.

Changing into the clothes, the daughter said, "I will always take care of my mom's pajamas."

And so, the Morning Motivation of today is, Mom's Pajamas.

Today family, go out and do good, every chance that you get. You never really know how your actions will affect someone else. It is better, I assume, to send positive energy, love, support, and comfort out into the world, so that others receive positive energy, love, support, and comfort.

And remember, you are awesome, you are amazing, you are wonderful, and you are great. And you, are gonna change the world. I just hope I'm still alive to see it, family.

I'm out. Good morning.

Book Twenty-Four

The Rain Cloud

Good morning. Good morning. Welcome back to Morning Motivation with Matthew Daniels, and today, I'm gonna tell you guys about, The Rain Cloud. That's right! The Rain Cloud. But what is Matthew Daniels talking about? Ummm...

A long, long time ago, in the land of Egypt, there was a Prince named Khamwas, and he was also the High Priest of Ptah at Memphis. The prince was a very learned scribe and magician who spent his time in the study of ancient monuments and books.

One day he was told of the existence of a book of magic written by the God Tehuti himself which was kept in the tomb of a Prince from the distant past. After a long and arduous search, Prince Khamwas, High Priest of Ptah, found the book of magic, which was written by the God Tehuti himself.

Excited beyond measure, he began to carefully unroll the ancient document. Ever so gently, the first sentences became clear.

"To... you... who are reading these words," the prince read out loud. "If this book has been passed down to you by one who deemed you worthy of having it, then use this book as you have been instructed. However, if you have merely found this book through searching, put it back, where you found it."

The prince laughed. "I am a prince and High Priest; I am more than worthy. Whether I searched or not."

Ignoring the warning, he turned to a spell called, The Rain Cloud. Intrigued by the name, he began to say the words of power, and recite the spell. Once he finished, right before his very eyes, a rain cloud appeared, no larger than a man, and it hovered and showered down rain in one spot.

The prince smiled.

"I am a great magician!" He exclaimed, turning to walk away.

BOOM!!

A loud clap of thunder rang out, and the prince turned around startled. The small rain cloud was growing and there was now thunder and lightning in addition to the rain.

The prince began frantically trying to find a spell to make the rain cloud go away, but he could not. Before he knew it, the rain cloud had outgrown the tomb and it covered the whole land of Egypt.

The rains fell, the land flooded, and the people suffered. After many days, the God Tehuti came and stopped the rain cloud, but the damage was already done.

And so, the Morning Motivation of today is, The Rain Cloud.

One of the hardest concepts for us to accept sometimes, is the fact that just because we 'can' do a thing, does not mean we 'should' do it. The ego, family, that thing that makes us feel entitled or deserving, can easily lead us into destruction.

That's why it must be kept in check. Consider the consequences of your actions and pay attention to the warning signs. One small situation can create several large situations, and things can quickly get out of hand.

Don't cheat your way to success, that way, you'll have no regrets.

And remember, you are awesome, you are amazing, you are wonderful, and you are great. And you, are gonna change the world. I just hope I'm still alive to see it, family.

I'm out. Good morning.

Book Twenty-Five

I Will Not Fail

Good morning. Good morning. Welcome back to Morning Motivation with Matthew Daniels, and today, I'm gonna tell you guys about, I Will Not Fail. That's right! I Will Not Fail. But what is Matthew Daniels talking about? Ummm...

A long, long time ago, somewhere inside of heaven, one of my ancestors overheard a conversation between two beings.

The first being said, "Every day we stand here and watch, as mankind destroys itself with its own wickedness. And as a consequence of this, the good, the righteous, and the upright, are slaughtered without cause. We listen to their children, call out, every second of every day. Their very blood yelling up to us from the ground upon which it was spilled. They are liars, cheats, murderers, and thieves. I have grown tired of the wickedness, and the suffering is all I can bear."

The second being, speaking in response said, "It would be my honor, to go on your behalf, and punish the wicked, and save the good."

"So be it." The first being said. "But you must first go down to them and endure what they have endured. And if you prevail, you may do what you wish with both the wicked and good."

With that, the second being went down into the earth to begin his trials, and my ancestor watched on in amazement.

My ancestor was not the only one watching. The tempter, he too, was keeping a close eye on these events.

And as soon as he heard that the second being had arrived on earth, the tempter unleashed his army of demons and devils. They began an attack on the second being, trying him at every turn. Trying with all of their wicked might, to break him down, so that he might quit.

The second being, being tortured physically and mentally, said to the Tempter.

"I am happy, that you have unleashed your worst on me. The extent to which you can cause mankind to suffer, is too great a burden for them to bear. Because of your wickedness to me, I am even more determined to overcome. And when I do, I will punish the wicked and save the good."

Then one day, the second being was in prayer.

"How long must I endure?" He asked. "Have I overcome enough?"

"No." The first being replied. "There is one more thing you must endure for them."

"Not my will, but yours be done." He answered.

"Go forth and endure death and trust in me."

With that, the second being went and tasted the sting of death, and gave up the ghost, like mankind does. But because of this, he was raised to new life, and he indeed, punished the wicked, and saved the good.

And so, the Morning Motivation of today is, I Will Not Fail.

Today family, imagine that you chose to come to earth for some noble cause, some righteous reason, and you are here to love, help, and live.

Now imagine that there are those who wish to stop you from achieving your goals. Do not be dismayed by their attacks. Instead, expect them. It comes with the mission. Yes, you will have to endure some things, some things you do not like. But you must achieve your dreams.

Tell yourself today, I Will Not Fail.

And remember, you are awesome, you are amazing, you are wonderful, and you are great. And you, are gonna change the world. I just hope I'm still alive to see it, family.

I'm out. Good morning.

Book Twenty-Six

God's Gamble

Good morning. Good morning. Welcome back to Morning Motivation with Matthew Daniels, and today, I'm gonna tell you guys about, God's Gamble. That's right! God's Gamble. But what is Matthew Daniels talking about? Ummm...

A long, long time ago, there was a man who lived in the land of Uz, whose name was Job, and this man was perfect and upright, and he feared God, and eschewed evil.

One day, for some reason, God was having a conversation with Satan, and he said, "Hast thou considered my servant Job, that there is none like him in the earth, a perfect and upright man, one that feareth God, and escheweth evil."

Satan replied by implying that Job was only faithful to God because of the blessings of protection, wealth, and family, that God had given him.

"If you were to put forth your hand now," Satan challenged. "And touch all that he hath, he will curse thee to thy face."

God then placed stipulations on the level of harm that Satan could bring to the righteous Job, but God allowed him to touch all that had.

Quickly, Satan went off to try and break Job's love for righteousness, and Job's love for God.

First, Satan whispered in the ear of the Sabeans, and persuaded them to murder the servants of Job, and take away his oxen and asses.

Next, Satan caused fire to fall from heaven, and consume Job's sheep, and the servants of Job who tended them.

Then, Satan convinced the Chaldeans to kill more of the servants of Job and take away his camels. Satan had launched an all-out assault on Job. An assault that even killed the sons and daughters of Job and covered his very body in boils and sores.

Yet, even in the face of all of this, Job did not lose his faith in God. Three friends of Job even came, and they proposed that perhaps Job himself were merely pretending to be righteous, and obviously God were punishing him for some serious sins.

Job and his friends debated what God was doing, and they all had different explanations for why God did to Job what He did, but neither of them assumed that it was a gamble.

Finally, growing tired of hearing them speak on His behalf and be wrong. God manifested before them in the form of a whirlwind.

"Who is this that darkeneth counsel by words without knowledge?" God called out. "Gird up now thy loins like a man; for I will demand of thee and answer thou me."

God then proceeded to ask them questions about the moments when he created the heavens and earth. And he questioned them about how he did it. God asked them about the animals and the elements, and He exposed their finite minds.

Then, God blessed Job by restoring all that he had lost two-fold. And God blessed the latter end of Job more than his beginning.

And so, the Morning Motivation of today is, God's Gamble.

Sometimes, the thing which God has planned for us, is connected to a plan that is too big for our human minds to comprehend. All we can do at times is be righteous, and maintain our faith in God, regardless of how hard we seem to have it.

Perhaps our struggles, were planned when God created the mountains, and they can not change. However, the purpose of the struggle isn't to struggle. The purpose is to bless you. So do good today, and hold onto your faith, and you will overcome.

And remember, you are awesome, you are amazing, you are wonderful, and you are great. And you, are gonna change the world. I just hope I'm still alive to see it, family.

I'm out. Good morning.

Book Twenty-Seven

The Seven Deadly Sins, Part One

Good morning. Good morning. Welcome back to Morning Motivation with Matthew Daniels, and today, I'm gonna tell you guys about, The Seven Deadly Sins, Part One. That's right! The Seven Deadly Sins, Part One. But what is Matthew Daniels talking about? Ummm...

A long, long time ago, in the area that we now call Florence, Italy, their lived a young man who was as curious as any other young man his age, and he would often explore the caves that sat a short distance from where he lived. The young man, being about 18 years old, had done this since about age 10, and he had just about explored every cave in the area.

One day, a mighty earthquake was unleashed upon the land, and when the young man returned to the caves after the event, he noticed that the earthquake had open up a cave system which he did not know existed. Excited over something new to explore, the young man immediately descended into the mouth of the cave.

His years of squeezing in and out of crevices allowed him to descend deeper and deeper, quite faster than a normal young man would. Suddenly feeling stuck, while crawling through a particularly tight space, the young man regulated his breathing, and contorted his body in such a way, that for a while, he was only being propelled forward by using his toes.

Through all of this, the young man did not lose his enthusiasm for his adventure. Indeed, the difficulty of it made it all the more enjoyable. Eventually, his persistence paid off. The passageway widened, and off in the distance, around a long curve, he could see a light.

Growing closer, the young man began to hear what sounded like the screeching of men and women. Their shrill cries sent chills down his spine. Pressing his back against the cool cave wall, the young man again regulated his breathing, and he began to slowly inch forward. As he did, the voices became horrendously clear. It was indeed men and women crying out in pain. Begging to be freed. Complaining about torture and begging for relief.

Fear, at once seized the young man's heart, and he turned to flee, but their was something else as well. Something deep within the young man that made him want to continue on his journey and see that which was producing such terrifying sounds.

"What manner of evil is that?" He wondered.

The young man stood inside of the cave for a moment and debated what he should do. Finally, he decided to press forward and see the sights that he had only heard until now. The young man then slowly and cautiously moved forward, edging closer and closer to the strange lights and the loud screams.

Reaching the end of the passageway, the young man approached a large opening that appeared to be lit by torches and flames. Gasping loudly, the young man saw a sea of men and women, all hooked up to a wretched type of machine. There were seven long lines with millions upon millions of people in them.

All of these men and women were being led to a wall with seven large doors.

The young man, in complete awe and amazement, looked on and said, "To be continued..."

And so, the Morning Motivation of today is, The Seven Deadly Sins, Part One.

Remember that patience is a virtue. And anything worth having is worth waiting for. Today family, I'm going to begin to take you on a literary journey. The likes of which, no writer, no author, no scribe, and no storyteller, has ever taken you on before. This is the intro family, be watching the page, you never know when part two will drop.

And remember, you are awesome, you are amazing, you are wonderful, and you are great. And you, are gonna change the world. I just hope I'm still alive to see it, family.

I'm out. Good morning.

Book Twenty-Eight

The Secret Word of Power

Good morning. Good morning. Welcome back to Morning Motivation with Matthew Daniels, and today, I'm gonna tell you guys about, The Secret Word of Power. That's right! The Secret Word of Power. But what is Matthew Daniels talking about? Ummm...

A long, long time ago, in the land of Egypt, around 500 years after the Gods and Goddesses had left planet earth, a young girl, who was in training to become a temple scribe was practicing her craft by copying some scrolls she found in one of the temples. After completing one scroll, she went over to the wall to choose another.

Finding one, which she thought would suit her purposes, she took the long rolled up scroll from its place on the shelf and carefully sat down on her mat on the floor. She then blew off a layer of dust and began to unroll the scroll.

As she did, there was a bright flash of a blinding light. When the young girl was able to see again, she saw the Goddess Aset standing in the room with her.

"Oh, Great Neteru Aset." The young girl exclaimed. "I am sorry if I disturbed you."

"On no, my child." Aset replied. "Do not be sorry, be happy. The Great One, Amen-Ra sealed me inside of that scroll over 500 years ago. I had made a snake which poisoned him, so that I might learn the secret word of power. And this was my punishment. For freeing me, I will give you the secret word of power. Say this word whenever you are in a challenging situation, and you will have all the powers of creation assisting you to succeed.

Then, there was another blinding flash of light, and Aset was gone. The young girl looked down at the scroll and there was only one word written. Astonished, the young girl snatched up the scroll and ran home. The next day, the young girl went to her teacher and said that she was ready to take her final exam to become an official temple scribe. Her teacher told her that her training was not yet complete, and if she took the test and failed, she would not be allowed to take the test a second time.

For to be a temple scribe, one must perfect the craft. She assured him that she was ready. She then closed her eyes, said the word of power, and began the test. After finishing it in record time, her teacher confirmed that she had successfully passed the test.

When he questioned how she had done this, she told him the story about Aset and showed him the scroll with the word of power on it. The teacher looked down at the scroll and smiled.

"Do you want to know what that word means?" He asked. Knowing it had not been used since the time of the Gods.

"Yes." The girl answered.

The teacher grinned even bigger, pointed down at the scroll, and said, "Confidence."

And so, the Morning Motivation of today is, The Secret Word of Power.

The Secret Word of Power is confidence, family. Today, you are going to believe in yourself. Today, you are going to conquer. Today you are going to succeed. No matter what obstacles you may face, as you journey on your day, if you would simply say the secret word of power... confidence; confidence in yourself and your abilities, then you will overcome.

And remember, you are awesome, you are amazing, you are wonderful, and you are great. And you, are gonna change the world. I just hope I'm still alive to see it, family.

I'm out. Good morning.

Book Twenty-Nine

The Crocodile, The Lion, The Snake, and Man

Good morning. Good morning. Welcome back to Morning Motivation with Matthew Daniels, and today, I'm gonna tell you guys about, The Crocodile, The Lion, The Snake, and Man. That's right! The Crocodile, The Lion, The Snake, and Man. But what is Matthew Daniels talking about? Ummm...

A long, long time ago, in the area that we call Africa today, there was a father and son who were taking a walk down a trail. And as they walked, they came upon a river, and they saw a crocodile resting on the bank. The son, intrigued, began to run over to the crocodile because he wanted to touch it.

The father yelled, "No." And stopped him.

Then he asked him why did he think it was ok to go over and touch such a dangerous creature. And the son said that he had seen crocodiles that were bigger and more ferocious than the crocodile that was resting, and so he did not think that it could hurt him very much.

And the father said that even though that crocodile was not the biggest and most ferocious crocodile that they had seen, it was still a crocodile, and it could still do as much damage as any other crocodile. While they were talking, an antelope walked over to the river to get something to drink, and the crocodile snatched it up, killed it, and ate it.

And so, the father and son continued to walk. As they walked, they came across a lion resting in the shade. The son, intrigued by the lion, ran over to touch it, and the father yelled "Stop!". The father had to again sit his son down and explain that even though that lion was not the biggest and most ferocious lion that they had ever seen, it was still a lion, and it could do just as much damage as any other lion.

While they were talking, a full-grown buffalo walked by and the lion pounced on him, killed him, and ate him. And so, the father and son continued to walk.

As they walked, they came across a black snake coiled up under a tree. The son, intrigued by the snake ran over to touch it, and the father yelled "Stop!" The father again sat his son down and explained that even though that snake wasn't the biggest and most ferocious snake that they had ever seen, it was still a snake, and it could do just as much damage as any other snake.

While they were talking, an even bigger snake slithered by, and the coiled up black snake attacked it, killed it, and ate it. After this, the father and son, went home, ate, and went to bed.

The next day the son was out in the field playing with the other children, and they were arguing and debating about which one of them should be the leader in the game they were playing.

And the son stood up and said, "I think that we should take turns being the leader. After all, a crocodile is a crocodile, a lion is a lion, a snake is a snake, and so, a man is a man. Any of us can have the capabilities to perform the task of the leader, so I think we should take turns."

All of the other children marveled at his wisdom, and they then made him the leader of their game. He eventually became the Chief and he went on to do great things in the village, because he never doubted his own abilities, nor the abilities of those around him.

And so, the Morning Motivation of today is, The Crocodile, The Lion, The Snake, and Man.

We all have people that we look up to, and we all have people that we admire. And we all have people that we feel have done great things. We all feel that there are people who do some things even better than we ourselves might be able do them.

But I want to remind you guys that you are human just like they are human, you have the same 24 hours in the day. You have the same capacity for learning. You have the same capacity for knowledge.

So now, anything that has been done, and anything that can be done, you can do it as well.

And remember, you are awesome, you are amazing, you are wonderful, and you are great. And you, are gonna change the world. I just hope I'm still alive to see it, family.

I'm out. Good morning.

Book Thirty

The Paradigm Shift

Good morning. Good morning. Welcome back to Morning Motivation with Matthew Daniels, and today, I'm gonna tell you guys about, The Paradigm Shift. That's right! The Paradigm Shift. But what is Matthew Daniels talking about? Ummm...

A long, long time ago, in a land which has since been destroyed by an enormous asteroid, there lived three brothers, who were so full of themselves, that they paid little to no attention to those around them. They felt entitled, set apart, and better than others.

These brothers had a rich and powerful father, who taught them to be ruthless in life and in business.

"Money." The father told them daily. "Is more important than men."

One day, these 3 brothers were walking through the forest when they stumbled upon a large tree, with what seemed to be a full-length mirror attached to it.

Intrigued by the site, the 3 brothers went over to inspect the tree.

"Look." One brother said. "The mirror is actually growing from the tree."

In complete awe and amazement, the brothers, ran their hands along the glass and the tree trunk, trying to see how a mirror could grow from a tree. As they inspected this wonder, they noticed in the mirror, 3 young boys walking towards them. Thinking these 3 young boys were actually behind them, the 3 brothers turned around.

Seeing no one, they turned their gaze back to the mirror, and they realized that the 3 young boys were somehow approaching them from inside of the mirror, and they stood and stared in wonder.

After a moment, the 3 boys reached the 3 brothers, and one of them said, "We have been trapped in this prison by our wicked and cruel father, since our birth. Can you break this glass, and free us, please?"

The 3 brothers replied, "What will you give us if we free you? We will not free you for free."

"We have nothing but our bodies and our lives." The 3 young boys pointed out. "We have nothing else to give."

The 3 brothers whispered amongst themselves.

"Very well, if you give us the bodies and lives of 2 of you, we will break the glass, and one of you may go free."

The jaws of the 3 boys dropped. They couldn't believe their ears.

"Would you really take 2 of us?" They asked, bewildered. "You could easily break the glass with that stick."

Shrugging their shoulders, the 3 brothers turned to walk away.

Horrified, the 3 boys called out.

"Wait! Wait! We agree! We agree! If you break the glass and free us, you may have the bodies and lives of 2 of us."

Smiling, the 3 brothers turned back, picked up the stick, and promptly smashed the glass. As soon as the 3 boys stepped through the broken glass, 2 of the brothers, and 2 of the young boys fell dead. Gasping, the 1 brother left alive asked what happened.

"I am you." The one boy left alive said. "And my 2 brothers were your 2 brothers. Our father placed us here with his teaching about life. You all had a chance to free us from this person, but instead, you've done this."

"Nooooo!" The one brother cried out.

And so, the Morning Motivation of today is, The Paradigm Shift.

Many of us are locked inside of mental prisons, placed on us by others. And we think that the way out of our condition is by sinking deeper into the unproductive mindset.

When really, to change your reality, you must change how you think, and change how you behave. Do that which is good, and you can easily shift your entire paradigm.

And remember, you are awesome, you are amazing, you are wonderful, and you are great. And you, are gonna change the world. I just hope I'm still alive to see it, family.

I'm out. Good morning.

Thank you for reading!

At this juncture in our motivational journey, I would like to thank you for reading this work. Quick question, dear reader, did you find anything of value within these pages? If so, be on the lookout for **Morning Motivation with Matthew Daniels volume 2**, which I have already begun writing.

Also, if you would like to hear me read these stories out loud, search out my social media pages.

TikTok: @matthewdaniels720

Facebook: Everything Matthew Daniels

YouTube: MatthewDaniels Tv

Cashapp: @TheRealBookWorm

Website: DandyandBigHerm.com

Well, dear reader, you know what they say. All good things must come to an end. So goodbye and have a great day. May your name live on forever, and may your memory never die.

Other Books by The Scribe Matthew Daniels

Suicide Note
Thicker Than Water
Big Game Hunting
My Beautiful and Loving Wife

All books by The Scribe Matthew Daniels are available on Amazon. Signed copies can be purchased from me directly. Visit DandyandBigHerm.com.

Made in the USA
Columbia, SC
11 April 2025